Happy Butterfly

by Pippa Goodhart

Illustrated by Lauren Tobia

W
FRANKLIN WATTS
LONDON • SYDNEY

First published in 2009 by
Franklin Watts
338 Euston Road
London
NW1 3BH

Franklin Watts Australia
Level 17/207 Kent Street
Sydney
NSW 2000

A CIP catalogue record for this book is available
from the British Library.

ISBN 978 0 7496 8513 3 (hbk)
ISBN 978 0 7496 8519 5 (pbk)

Series Editor: Jackie Hamley
Editor: Melanie Palmer
Series Advisor: Dr Hilary Minns
Series Designer: Peter Scoulding

Printed in China

Franklin Watts is a division of
Hachette Children's Books,
an Hachette UK company.
www.hachette.co.uk

Happy heard a band.
"I want to see it!"
she said.

Just then a butterfly
flew down in front
of Happy.

Then it flew up again.

"Lucky butterfly!"
said Happy.

"Would you like to be a butterfly?" asked Grandma Gloria.

Grandma took Happy shopping.

They got wire
and netting.

They got sparkles.

They got beads.

Grandma Gloria made wings.

Happy stuck on sparkles and beads.

They made a head
band together.

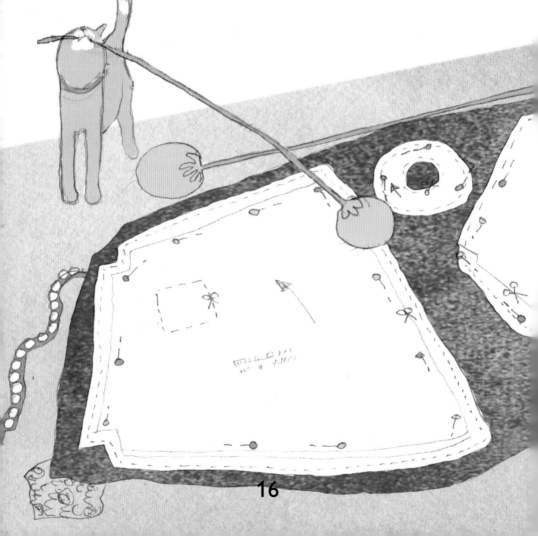

17

"Look at me, I'm a butterfly!" said Happy.

This time, Happy saw everything!

21

Puzzle Time!

a
b
c
d
e
f

Put these pictures in the right order and retell the story!

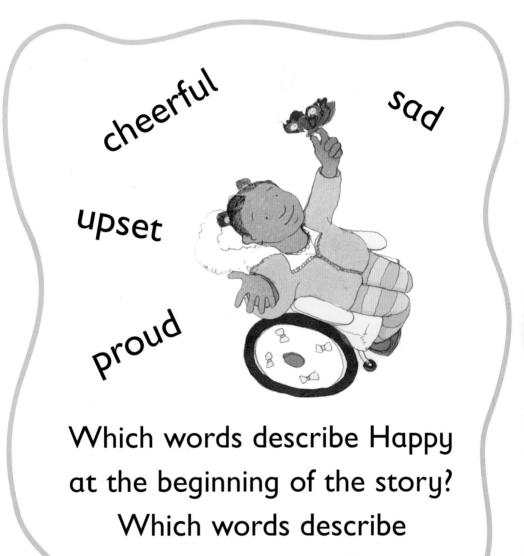

cheerful

sad

upset

proud

Which words describe Happy
at the beginning of the story?
Which words describe
her at the end?

Turn over for answers!

Notes for adults

Answers

Here is the correct order!

1.d 2.e 3.f 4.a 5.c 6.b

Words to describe Happy at the beginning:
sad, upset

Words to describe Happy at the end:
cheerful, proud